The Bamboo Cutter's Daughter

A Traditional Tale from Japan
Retold by Lynette Evans
Illustrated by Yukari Kakita

Japan

Takesh lives in the beautiful,
bustling city of Kyoto. As a
young child, his grandmother
would often take him and
his sisters to one of Kyoto's
many rock gardens, where
she would tell them wonderful
stories. The tale
of the Bamboo
Princess was
one of their
favorites.

蓬萊山

竜宮

In this age-old tale from Japan, we read about a beautiful and gentle princess who put the needs of others before herself and whose *kindness* was greater than any in the land.

kindness helping others

The Bamboo Princess

The evening shadows were growing long as the weary
bamboo cutter made his way home. Farther down the path,
among the stalks of feathery bamboo, he saw a soft light.
It seemed to be shining from within one of the stalks.

    The old man rubbed his eyes, thinking that his long,
hard day at work was causing him to imagine things,
but still the soft light shone. He opened the bamboo stalk
very carefully. There, nestled in the heart of the stalk, was
a tiny girl. She was as delicate and as beautiful as a fairy.

The bamboo cutter was greatly surprised. Gently, he picked up the tiny girl and carried her home to show his wife. The old couple were overjoyed. They had no children, so they took care of the little fairy girl and raised her as their own. They named her the Bamboo Princess because she was found among the bamboo. In time, the Bamboo Princess grew into a beautiful young woman whose looks were matched only by her kind heart and her sweet nature.

overjoyed *very happy*

Before long, tales about the kindness and beauty of the Bamboo Princess spread across the land. People came from near and far to catch a glimpse of her as she tended the flowers and trees in her parents' garden.

Word of the Bamboo Princess even reached the royal palaces, and many young princes came to see her. There were five, in particular, who could not stay away. Each one thought the Bamboo Princess the most beautiful woman he had ever seen, and each one wished to have her as his wife.

As was the custom, each of the young princes wrote a letter to the bamboo cutter, asking permission to marry his daughter. It so happened that all five letters were brought to the old man at the very same time.

The bamboo cutter didn't know which prince to choose. He was afraid that if he chose one, the other four would be angry. "Have them all come here, Father," the Bamboo Princess said. "That way, we can make the wisest choice."

On the chosen day, the five princes arrived, each one confident that he would be the special one. The truth, however, was that the Bamboo Princess did not wish to marry at all. She wished to stay and take care of her dear mother and father. So she gave each of the princes an impossible task.

custom a traditional way of doing things

The Impossible Tasks

To the first prince, she said:
To show your true love for me, you must go to India and bring me the Great Stone Bowl of Buddha.
To read about this adventure, turn to page 10.

To the second prince, she said:
To show your true love for me, you must go to the floating mountain of Horai and bring me a branch from a jewel tree that grows there.
To read about this adventure, turn to page 14.

To the third prince, she said:
To show your true love for me, you must bring me a robe made from the skins of the dreaded fire rats.
To read about this adventure, turn to page 18.

To the fourth prince, she said:
To show your true love for me, you must bring me the shell that the swallows keep hidden and guarded in their nest.
To read about this adventure,
turn to page 22.

To the fifth prince, she said:
To show your true love for me, you must bring me a jewel from the necklace of the great sea dragon that sleeps beneath the waves.
To read about this adventure,
turn to page 26.

The five princes hurried away. Each one was anxious to be the first to complete the task that the Bamboo Princess had set. Then he could be the one to marry the Bamboo Princess.

The Great Stone Bowl

People say that hidden in the darkness of an ancient temple in the heart of India, there lies a stone bowl that once belonged to the great spiritual teacher, Buddha. Legend has it that the Great Stone Bowl sparkles and glows with the fire of rubies and precious gems of all colors. Few have ever laid eyes on the stone bowl, but those who have cannot stop talking about its beauty.

Now the prince who promised to journey to India in search of the Great Stone Bowl was, in fact, a very lazy man. It is true to say that when he stood before the Bamboo Princess, he really did mean to do the job, but somehow the more he thought about the journey, the lazier he felt. In his heart of hearts he began to wonder if he really should bother at all.

The prince gathered his most experienced sailors and asked them how long it would take to journey to India and back again. When they told him he would spend three years on the quest for the Bamboo Princess, he decided once and for all that he would not go. He wasn't about to waste years of his life searching for some old bowl! Instead, he went to live in a nearby city for three years.

quest an adventurous journey to find something

Then, it is sad to say, the prince did something that no prince should ever do! At the end of the three years, he crept into a little temple in a quiet corner of the city. There, lying dusty and forgotten, was an old stone bowl. The prince took this bowl and wrapped it in cloth made of the finest silk and embroidered with threads of gold.

The prince then wrote a letter, telling the Bamboo Princess about his long, adventurous journey to India and the hardships he had faced. He told her how tirelessly he had worked to find the bowl. Then he sent the letter to her.

The Bamboo Princess almost wept as she read the letter. She was sorry that the prince had suffered so much to bring her the bowl. Then she opened the silk wrapping and saw the bowl of common stone. She knew then that the prince had tried to trick her, and her pity turned to anger. She returned the bowl and refused to see him.

The prince felt sad, but he knew that he deserved it. He kept the bowl to remind him of an important lesson: *Good comes to those who are honest and hard-working.*

honest truthful

The Branch of the Jewel Tree

People say that in a land far, far away, there is a floating mountain called Horai. Legend has it that trees of gold grow on the floating mountain. The golden trees have branches studded with leaves made of precious jewels that glisten and gleam in the magical mists. Few have ever found their way to the floating mountain, but those who have cannot stop talking about the jewel trees.

Now the prince who promised to bring back a branch from one of the jewel trees was, in fact, a very cunning and rich man. He did not believe that there was a floating mountain called Horai, and he did not believe that there were trees of gold with jewels for leaves. However, he had stood before the Bamboo Princess and promised to journey to the floating mountain. So the prince said farewell to his friends and went down to the seashore.

It was three years before anyone saw or heard of the prince again. Then, one day, he appeared at the home of the old bamboo cutter and his wife and asked to see the Bamboo Princess. The prince carried before him a most wonderful branch of gold. On the branch were delicate blossoms and jeweled leaves of many colors.

The Bamboo Princess asked the prince to tell his story.

cunning   clever in a way that uses tricks and dishonesty

"There are no maps to show the way to the floating mountain," the prince said, "so I let the wind and the waves carry me across the seas. We passed many strange countries and beautiful cities. We saw great sea dragons lying on the water, sleeping as the waves rocked them. We saw sea serpents coiling on the sea floor. And above us flew birds with the bodies of animals.

At times, fierce storms turned the waves into mountains of water, and wild winds drove us into unknown lands. At other times, we floated with not even a breath of wind to move us for weeks. We ran out of food and water, and just when I thought we could survive no longer, there before us rose the great mountain from the sea.

We landed, and I broke this branch off the mountain's most beautiful tree. A steady wind was blowing, so we set sail for home right away. I came directly from the ship to bring you this."

Tears welled up in the eyes of the Bamboo Princess as she thought of how greatly the prince had suffered to bring her the branch of the jewel tree. Before she could speak, however, there came a loud knocking at the door.

Three men stood outside. They were thin with hunger and dressed poorly. "We come in search of the prince," they said. "We want to be paid for our years of hard work."

The prince began to drive the men away, but the Bamboo Princess told them to stay. "What do you mean?" she asked.

"For three years, we have been working down by the seashore to make this beautiful, golden branch for the prince. Now that it is finished, we want our money."

The prince was ashamed. He knew the Bamboo Princess would never believe in him now.

She gave the jewel branch to the workmen as payment, and they praised her for her kindness.

ashamed   feeling guilty

The Fire Robe

People say that somewhere in the great land of China, there is a robe that shines with a brightness unlike any other garment ever made. Legend has it that this beautiful robe is made of the fur of the fierce and dreaded fire rats and that each time the robe is cast into the bright flames of a fire, it comes out more radiant than ever before. In all the years that people have spoken of the fire robe, however, no one has ever found it.

Now the prince whose task it was to find the fire robe was not only wealthy, but he was also a kind and much loved man. Prince Abe had friends in many parts of the world, including one very dear friend who was a great lord in China. To this friend, he sent a bag heavy with gold and a letter asking for his help in finding the mysterious fire robe.

When the friend in China read the letter, he grew sad, for the task ahead seemed almost impossible, and he did not want to disappoint his friend. Because he was such a loyal friend, however, he was determined to help Prince Abe. So he sent out messengers to search the land. He spoke with merchants who traveled far and wide. He questioned every priest at every temple. The reply was always the same: no one knew where the fire robe was hidden.

loyal faithful

One day, an old beggar man limped up to the lord and knelt before him. "My lord, when I was a child, my grandfather told a story about this fire robe," he said. "He saw the beautiful robe with his own eyes. It was kept in a temple on top of a mountain far from here."

The lord sent messengers to search for the mountain, and the old beggar went with them. When they arrived there, they found a pile of fallen stones. Beneath the stones they found a large iron box, and in the iron box, wrapped in many folds of rich silk, they found a strange and most beautiful fur robe.

Prince Abe was delighted when he received the parcel from China. "I will put the robe in the fire once again so that it may be more dazzling for the Princess than it has ever been before," he said to himself.

Prince Abe laid the silver robe over some burning coals. In a flash, hungry flames leaped up, and before he could snatch it away, there was nothing left of the robe but silvery ashes and smoke drifting on the wind.

Poor Prince Abe was heartbroken. He did not blame his faithful friend, for he had done his best. Instead, the prince was thankful that he had not taken the robe to the Bamboo Princess in case she thought that he, too, meant to trick her. He decided to write to her and tell her the truth. Then he would leave, for he had failed in his task.

The Bamboo Princess was sad when she read the letter, for she saw that this prince was honest and full of courage.

courage bravery

20

The Shell in the Swallow's Nest

People tell a story about a shell that lay hidden in the soft feather lining of a swallow's nest built high into the eaves of a magnificent palace. Although the shell did not start out with any great magical powers, it is true to say that through it, people have learned a lesson to this day.

The story began with the prince who was given the task of finding the shell in the swallow's nest. This prince was a proud and impatient young man who often had more than a little trouble controlling his temper.

When the prince returned from his visit with the Bamboo Princess, he called his chief servant to him. "Do you know anything about the shell that the swallows keep hidden in their nest?" he asked. "I want that shell immediately."

The chief servant asked the gardener, and the gardener asked the water carrier, but not one of them knew where the shell was to be found. Soon all the servants of the house had been asked, but still no one knew.

At last, the servants asked the children. One little boy said he had seen a shell once. He had been up on the kitchen roof looking for swallows' eggs and thought he saw a shell in one of the nests.

impatient unable to wait for things

The prince ordered his servants to search the swallows' nests on the kitchen roof. They returned complaining that the nests were too high and out of reach.

"You must find a way to reach them," roared the prince. "Do not dare return until you have searched every nest."

The servants spent three days trying to climb up. At last they attached a basket to a rope and pulled a man up so he could look into the nests, but still they found no shell.

When the servants told the prince, he fell into a rage. "I will see for myself," he shouted angrily.

The prince sprang into the basket and demanded that he be pulled up at once. When he reached the nests, the swallows began to peck fiercely at him. They did not want to have all their eggs broken and their nests ripped apart.

"Help! Help!" screamed the prince. As the servants began to lower the basket, he put his hand into one of the nests and felt something hard. Then he lost his balance and tumbled out of the basket and landed with a crash and a thump.

The servants helped the prince to his feet. He was covered with bruises. In one hand he held a shell—but it was only a jagged piece of eggshell, and egg was splattered all over his hands and face.

The prince decided then and there that he would forget about the shell and forget about the Bamboo Princess, but he did not forget the lesson he learned. From that day, he had a great respect for the swallows and never climbed up to peep into birds' nests again!

respect   to admire and be considerate of others

The Sea Dragon's Jewel

People say that far beneath the turquoise waves there lies a great sea dragon that sleeps on the golden sands of the sea floor. Like all dragons, this monster of the deep guards a *hoard* of gold and gems that glow in the underwater darkness. Around his thick, scaly neck he wears the most beautiful jewel of all. Legend has it that the dragon can command the wind to whip up fierce storms and crashing waves should anyone try to steal his treasure.

hoard   a large quantity of treasure that is hidden away

Now the prince whose task it was to fetch the sea dragon's jewel was, in fact, a terrible boaster and a complete coward. He wanted to bring the magnificent jewel to the Bamboo Princess, but you can be sure that he did not plan on doing the job himself.

Instead, he called his servants and soldiers together and gave them plenty of money to complete the task. While they were away, the prince set about building the most beautiful palace for the Bamboo Princess, for he did not doubt that he would be the one to marry her.

boaster   a person who talks about himself in a prideful way

The servants and soldiers took the money, but they did not bother to search for the sea dragon. They didn't believe that there was such a monster, and if there was, they certainly didn't want to risk waking him up.

The prince waited for a year, but still no one returned with the jewel. He became angry and decided at last that he would go himself. The servants who were left begged him not to go. They were afraid that the sea dragon would destroy them all.

"Cowards!" cried the prince. "Learn how to be brave from me. Do you think I am afraid of a sleepy dragon?"

After three days on the water, a fierce storm came up. The boat rocked and dipped. Great waves crashed over the side, lightning flashed, and thunder roared. The prince turned green with fear and seasickness.

"It must be the sea dragon that sends this storm," the servants said. "Perhaps you should promise not to steal his treasure, and our lives will be spared."

So the prince promised to leave the sea dragon alone, and the waves were still. When they landed on a nearby island, the prince was so happy to be on solid ground that he decided never to leave it—not for a hundred princesses!

The Moon Maiden

The years passed, and the Bamboo Princess took good care of her father and mother. Over time, she grew more beautiful and kind, but she also began to be very sad. She wept because although she had been sent to take care of the old bamboo cutter and his wife, her home was really in the moon, and her time on earth was coming to an end. She knew that on the next full moon, her father and mother would die, and she would return to her home in the sky.

Nothing could stop the passing of time. Each day, the new moon grew fuller and fuller until slowly, over the tops of the trees on the mountain, there rose a great silver ball. A line of light like a fairy bridge stretched from the moon to the earth, and down it came an army of soldiers in shining armor.

The leader laid the old couple to rest among the bamboo. Then he gently placed a beautiful silk cloak around the Bamboo Princess, and sure enough, she became a moon maiden once more.

Rising like the morning mists that lie along the lake, the soldiers marched with the moon maiden to the top of Fujiyama, the sacred mountain of Japan. Then they rose until they reached the silver gates of the moon city.

People say that a soft, white trail of smoke rises from Fujiyama like a floating bridge to that city in the sky where the Bamboo Princess lives in happiness and peace forever.

Discussion Starters

1. Each one of the princes had strengths and weaknesses. Which prince do you think most deserved to marry the Bamboo Princess? Why? Which prince do you think behaved the worst?

2. The Bamboo Princess is so kind and beautiful, she seems almost too good to be true! Do you think anyone could be so perfect in real life? Why or why not?

The Bamboo Princess was very kind to give up so much to take care of her parents. What would you have done if you had been her?